BLOOD ON ORCHARD STREET

A Fiction Based Crime Novel

CHARLES MORST

Order this book online at www.trafford.com
or email orders@trafford.com

Most Trafford titles are also available at major online book retailers.

Printed in the United States of America.

ISBN: 978-1-4907-0776-1 (sc)
ISBN: 978-1-4907-0775-4 (e)

Trafford rev. 08/22/2013

Trafford PUBLISHING®   www.trafford.com

North America & international
toll-free: 1 888 232 4444 (USA & Canada)
fax: 812 355 4082

Special Thanks To:

My beautiful and strong wife, who has been there from the very beginning
Supported me the whole way through this journey
Life would not be the same without
Her love and devotion
I Love You

To my two wonderful, children Jaiden and A'niya
To show them that every dream and goals
Is worth reaching for and that there is no
Road that is too long to reach the end

A Very Special Thank You to My Publication

And a Huge Thanks To All the Supportive Readers. These books are for
the crime lovers and suspense seekers. A good read for a great day. Enjoy!

To The Reader:

The purpose of this book it to give the reader a thrilling and suspenseful read into a world of crime. The first book in the *Fierce 8* collection of short fiction based crime novels, Author *Charles Morst* brings you crime stories sure to please. This book in dedicated to the readers. Thanks you for all your support and

I hope you enjoy!

PART 1

BLOOD ON ORCHARD STREET

It was Saturday morning in the south end of the city. There were lawns full of rocks and footprints where children had played hop-scotch and follow-the-leader. It was a quiet day, but for the local police districts and other our law enforcement agents it was a "day of murder". It seemed like when you were in the eyes of darkness that was all you saw. I had spent ten years on the force, and I still couldn't get use to it.

I remembered back when I first started, and I had my first couple of cases. I would go home to the horrible truth that when I lied down I wouldn't sleep, but relive the nightmare. I would dream of a lonely girl, a flying bullet, and a smile from a beautiful painting that would never be painted again. I didn't know how others dealt with this kind of pain. I had wished for the strength to deal with it, but I had always hoped that it would just change.

As I arose from the bed, body feeling cold, I made my way to the kitchen to eat whatever meal would be possible before the next patrol call came in, or the next rescue mission that involved us diving out of buildings to secure hostages. Just then phone rang, and I was drawn to Brandon's picture flashing across the screen. "Brandon, I wondered what he could need this early?" I thought as I took a sip of the orange juice I poured fresh from the ice box. "Hello Brandon," I said, "Good Morning Mike, What going on in Mikey land," Brandon said giggling, like there were admission tickets to a real amusement park. Brandon was always a joker, and I guess I had gotten used to the humor. Brandon was a sharp, young twenty-four years old detective, who had been on the force for six years. He had transferred from a small, city precinct a couples hundred miles away. He didn't know his parents growing up, and being that I grew up an orphan, we became the best of friend. I guess you could say we clicked. He had been my partner for the last four years and we made the best team. By now, I knew that our morning routine always led us to a morning stroll in the park to clear our heads from the night before. "So park in twenty minute, old friend," I said. Of course, he said the response I expected.

After a quick shower, shoving a biscuit into my mouth and drinking the rest of the orange juice I had poured. It was just what I needed to start the day. I grabbed the key to the new, black, vintage Mustang, which I received at a promotion party for nine years of outstanding performance in the Homicide unit. I picked up my coat and quickly made haste down a set of old, brown, wooden steps. My phone rang yet again. It was another call from Brandon. "Hello," I answered, waiting for Brandon to reply. "Hey Mike, meet me at the bench by the water fountain," he said. I quickly replied and hung up the phone as I opened the door to my vehicle.

Fifteen to twenty minutes later I pulled up to the park and swung around the outskirt as I tried to spot where Brandon had park his classic, muscle car? I looked off to the side of the water fountain just beyond the falling water and spotted him standing there. His eyes drifting as he stared off. I parked and walked up to Brandon. "Hey Brandon, how are you doing," I said slowly. "What going on, old friend" Brandon said to me glaring off into the sun.

The water fountain was a very popular spot for locals and soon the park was crawling with people! There were stores running along the

2

park's outskirt. There was Ms. Anderson pet shop along with Mr. Wilson flower seed and plant shop, and many others. After we chatted for a quick second, we began our walk around the park.

We were soon approached by Ms. Peterson and her sixteen year old son, Billy. "Yooo Hooo Mike, how do you do!," she said, walking fast in her flower, cuffed dress with a white, scarf wrapped around her neck. A bright, red lipstick softly glazed across her lips and a soft, coat of powder foundation giving her face a fine, upscale look. "Well hello there Ms. Peterson, what a pleasure," I spoke with a sound of interest. "Hello Ms. Peterson," said Brandon. "Hello, how are you doing, Brandon," said Ms. Peterson as she brushed her hair back.

She taped little Billy on the shoulder and shoved him forward. "Say hello Billy," she stated. Billy fixing his lips to open as his hands sweated from the grip of hers and his left eye began to twitch. "Hello Mr. Mike and Mr. Brandon," he said softly. Billy was a blue eyed, black haired young child who was soft spoken and quiet. He was shy growing up and always with his mother. He had recently attended the local school a few years until he became ill, so he was home bound for a while. As sweet as he was I believed he needed to get out more.

He wasn't a big social butterfly, and I felt it would be healthy to meet more kids. Ms. Peterson was a recent widow. Her late husband, Grant Tollson, was the founder and president of an oil company. She was a sweet, petite woman who came from the south. She was in her early forties and was very social from what I knew. There were rumors she had dated several men in the city and she was very active in the community. She been living here for a while before I transferred to this precinct and despite the rumors, she was a wonderful woman who made pies for the churches fruit festivals. "Well, what you doing in these fine parts Ms. Peterson," I stated as I swayed my body back and forth. "Oh, Nothing much, just taking Billy around town to see the upcoming festival flyers. We're getting ready to get down!" said Ms. Peterson. Brandon scratching the back of his head," Sounds like fun Ms. Peterson" With the time passing we knew that we needed to get to the office before the Captain called us in.

We decided to cut the conversation short and took off. We made our way to Third Avenue where the police In-process Unit was located, so we could begin our rounds As Brandon and I headed in to gear up and check in with the squad. The Tactic and Special Mission agents informed us about a call, Captain Waters wanting us on . . . ASAP! We acknowledged and headed to the Captain office for the rundown. As we enter the Captain's office, he sat there eyes tight as always whenever we got a call. The call that always hit hard, but at this point, we expected them.

"Yes Captain, you needed to see us," I said sitting down waiting for the Captain to give us the news. "Boys, we just got a call regarding a shooting on Orchard Street, and I need you guys to go check it out," the Captain said. "Orchard Street! We were just over there," said Brandon. As I sat there wondering what happened. "Ms. Peterson was shot," the Captain informed us. We were shocked from the news regarding the shooting of Ms. Peterson. We had just left her at the park. "I need to guys to cover this one," the Captain stated. "We're on it Captain!"

As Brandon and I headed back to what was now the scene of the crime. We began canvassing the area to see if there were any witnesses or if there was anyone that had possible details that would help us figure out what happened. We decided to split up and meet back up at the pub down the road once we interviewed the town folks around the crime scene. Thirty minutes later, Brandon walked into the pub as I sat there drinking a glass of despair. The same glass I always drunk to engulf myself. That was how I handled the scenes and stories that every victim told. "Can I get a double on the rock?" Brandon shouted out as he pulled up a stool and took a deep breath.

I had reached down into my side pocket to retrieve my interview notes and compare them with Brandon notes he collected from the town folks. "So what did you come up with?" I asked. Brandon reached into his cargo pocket to retrieve his notes as he took a sip of his drink. "As much as I was able to get my hand on," he muttered. After several drinks, Brandon and I had compared notes and discussed the theory of what we believed might have happened and discuss the facts we knew. Based on what the crime lab had presented from the first initial evidence run, and from what the locals stated had happened at about nine 'o' clock a.m. This would have been around the time we left the water fountain to head in to the office.

Ms. Peterson and her son left to see the festival flyers. From the time we left them to head to the office and got the call in from the Captain, an hour or so had passed. So between this time Ms. Peterson and her son had traveled several places throughout town to see the flyers and headed back to Orchard Street. About this time, reports from locals stated that gunshots were heard. Reports stated that there were two shot fired and in addition, we believed Ms. Peterson's son, Billy, was not around at the time. I wonder if this was a random hit and kidnapping or was this personal. She did recently inherit a large lump sum of money and a life insurance policy of over one million dollars split within the estate of her late husband.

The clock was ticking, and we were determined to find out what happened? Brandon and I reviewed the initial hard evidence from the crime lab while we waited for the autopsy report. The evidence showed the two gunshots to the victim's body. One shot to the victim's chest and one shot to the victim's lower stomach region. The shots were caused by a nine millimeter handgun. Evidence also showed that the shots were projected close range, so the person was somebody that Ms. Peterson knew. Later that night, we decided to canvas the street for more evidence or details that would explain the crime. We knew Ms. Peterson and her son were walking in town so there must have been an eye witness and we needed to locate where little Billy was.

I had called down to the precinct to see if any officers had driven out to the house. "We are swamped down here Mike, you guys are going to have to check it out," the Captain stated. I suspected that no one had thoroughly secured the victim's home. Brandon and I jumped in our cars and headed to the Peterson's home. As we pulled up to the house, we noticed that the back lights were on.

Now I knew Ms. Peterson for a number of years, and I know she never left the lights on. Somebody was in the house. I flagged Brandon to the right side as I took the left and we flanked up the siding of the house. As I slowly scouted the area for clues that would indicate who was inside, I noticed the side door.

I begun to hear what sounded like cartoons. I quickly saw Brandon setup in to position as he approached the door alongside me. He knew we were going in full force. As we prepare for entry, I wonder who could be in the home. Ms. Peterson lived alone with her son, and I knew of no out of town visitors. And as for Billy, he was missing. It was time to shed some light to this puzzle. I signal Brandon to move on three and kicked the door in. "EEKKK," a voice shouted as we entered the room guns raised and eyes red from lack of sleep.

As Brandon and I quickly scanned the room we looked toward the couch to see who was watching television. It was Billy sitting there shaking from the shock of our unexpected entry. "What are you doing here, Billy?" I say curiously. "I'm waiting on my mother to get back. She dropped me off earlier, and ran back out to pick something up from the flower shop," Billy replied. He didn't know what had happened.

This young helpless boy's mother shot down in cold blood by someone close to her. So she went to the flower shop. Mr. Wilson's Flower Shop was one of the places we had not yet checked out. I knew little of Mr. Wilson. He was a short, chubby man who prayed that the little bit of hair, and plants he had would grow this summer. He was kind and I never had a problem out of Mr. Wilson. He called on some occasions if there were teenagers bothering his store, but nothing major. I knew we couldn't leave Billy all alone, so I figure we would take him to the office and see what the Captain wanted to do. There was not much family for Billy to stay with at this point. I wanted to swing by Mr. Wilson's Flower Shop before he shut down for the day. It was starting to get late and he closed the shop early nowadays, and we still had to drop Billy off somewhere.

I instructed Brandon to take him on down to the station, while I went to see Mr. Wilson.

We went our separate way and twenty minute later I pulled up to Mr. Wilson's Flower Shop. "Evening Detective, what can I do for you," said Mr. Wilson turning his head as he placed flower pots outside his door. "Evening Mr. Wilson, I wonder if I could have a word," I said. "Why of course Detective, I see no problem with that," he happily replied. I began to ask Mr. Wilson about earlier events leading up to the time of the murder.

What he had been doing all day and if he had saw Ms. Peterson before the murder. According to Mr. Wilson, earlier in the day he observed me and Detective Brandon speaking with Ms. Peterson at the water fountain. After our short talk and we took our leave, Mr. Wilson stated, he saw a man approach Ms. Peterson, hug her and then walk toward Baker Street.

He said the man was not familiar to him. "Anything else you can remember?" I replied after a brief pause. He also stated that afterward, as he was watering the back roses. He heard a loud stiff of chatter coming from the street. As he was walked around to see what was going on. Gunfire erupted and he saw a figure running off in to the dark siding of some trees. "Thank you Mr. Wilson, you have been a great help," I replied to the wonderful information he provided. I had found an eye witness and even though he didn't see the shooter face, thankfully I have more to go on. "Have a good day Mr. Wilson," I shouted out.

I returned to my car to go over what course of action to take next. As I started the car getting ready to press the gas my phone rang. It was Brandon calling from the office. "Hey Mike, Captain Waters needs you back at the office, and we are taking Billy to the neighbor," Brandon informed me. "I'm on my way back now," I said hanging up and laying my books on the seat. Shortly after the interview with Mr. Wilson, when I returned to the precinct to take care of what needed to be done, and grabbed a quick bite to eat. I was informed by the local Coroner's

Office that the DNA results were in and that the autopsy was finished. The Coroner had explained to me that on the victim's clothes DNA from her son was found which would just prove that her son was around her. And we knew that Billy was with his mother all day before he was dropped off.

The crime lab showed gun residue on the victim's clothes from the two gunshots. In addition, other forensics showed fingerprints on the victim's back. There were also strands of hairs found on the victim's body. With any luck, we would be able to send the DNA and hair samples up to the Regional lab for more analysis and get more clear information on our evidence. Depending on the Coroner's workload, the lab turnaround time on evidence testing was pretty quick. We had to find out who our mystery man, Ms. Peterson met in the park was. He was the key to finding out more information on the events before the murder. I met up with Brandon in the Captain's Office to be briefed on the next task.

"Good work gathering information detectives. I need for you guys to take Billy to the neighbors. They are willing to take custody of him for the time being until we can place him in the care of family," the Captain informed us. "Also I need for Billy to do a statement of what he and his mother were doing before he was dropped off". "Ok Captain, we will take care of everything and report back in," Brandon replied.

As Brandon and I left the precinct to take Billy to the residence that he would be staying at for a while, we needed to do some more research on why Ms. Peterson was brutally murder, and find out what the motives could have been that caused someone to kill her. It was awful nice of the neighbor to take Billy in. It was around one 'o'clock am, and they were willing to open their door and welcome us into their home. We brought Billy's bags in, showed our gratitude and made our way back to our vehicle. As Brandon and I sat there in the car for a second to gather our thoughts, I wondered what the criminal was doing. Had the suspect thought we given up or that we wouldn't catch him or her?

The suspect always got to comfortable and made a mistake somewhere. "We need to start looking for a murder weapon since forensic didn't find one," I stated.

We decided to go back and scout the area and possibly head to the Peterson's residence that was now surrounded with police caution tape. At the original scene of the crime, Brandon and I looked for any kind of unnoticeable evidence that might have slid its way passed forensics' keen, eye for weirdness. In the midst of our search Brandon and I set up a perimeter to double check the areas that were secured off earlier by crime specialists and the Coroner's team. Off in the distance I noticed a chipped piece of metal. It was probably nothing and that why it wasn't bagged, but in a murder investigation you must consider all evidence as strong or supportive evidence.

I called Brandon over to take a look. "Hey Brandon, what you suppose this is?" I asked. Brandon nodded and squinted. "Looks like pieces of a metal band or something?" he replied. It could be something and I decided to take it just in case. We headed to the home to search for any documents that would lead us in the right direction for a motive. In the home, Brandon found several life insurance papers and a will with lines to the recipient's paragraph awarded Billy the sole trustee at the age of eighteen scratched out. It would seem that the criminal knew that she had this inheritance, and maybe tried to alter the paper to be the one to receive the money upon final transfer. We may have found our motive, but it was only a theory. We had found pieces of chipped metal and insurance forms, but what was our next piece to solving this murder.

We decided to call it a day. We had been at it all night, and I felt it was a success. We headed back to the station to report in to Captain Waters. We had not found a murder weapon or the man that Ms. Peterson saw earlier that day. Even though we were moving slow in the process, things were looking up. I needed more results from the crime lab, and I would have a little more to work with.

The next day as the sun slowly made it way up and gave the world its morning cup of coffee. I was knee deep in paperwork as I tried to recap my thoughts. I had completely side tracked myself and forgot to get Billy's statement. I paged Brandon so we could get to work and I washed up. I headed out to the office. "Morning partner," I said, greeting Brandon at the breezeway. "Good Morning, you sleep ok?" Brandon asked as he strapped his belt clip. Brandon nodded and smiled.

I guess you could tell by my face if I had slept well. We headed to the Captain's Office to get briefed and obtain more information. "Boys, we got the results from the Regional crime lab. Also, I got word from local field police that we have a suspect in custody. A man was spotted in Ms. Peterson's backyard. He might be our mystery man that was with Ms. Peterson," he suggested. After our briefing with the Captain, Brandon and I went to gear up and waited as the patrol officers brought in the suspect for questioning.

The man was rough and smelled of cheap cologne. His clothes were tattered like he'd had been attacked. The officer placed the man in the interrogation room. Brandon and I entered the room and sat down cautiously. "Good Morning sir, my name is Detective Mike Hallman. I am the Lead Homicide Detective, and this is my partner Detective Brandon Small. "Do you know why you are here sir," I stated as I sat down opening up my books to write down notes. "No! He shouted. He stated that he was looking for Ms. Peterson. The man stated that he hadn't heard from her in weeks. And the only thing that he could recall was the night they had dinner at Sue's Grill House.

I stayed in the room while Brandon checked out the man's alibi. Minutes later, Brandon returned to verify that the man's story had checked out. We had no choice but to let him go. We kept the man identity wrapped from the media, but I wondered if there was more to the story. For now, he was a dead lead and I needed to check out more avenues.

There were still the results at the lab. I figure Brandon, and I should head down to the lab and get the information on what the Regional crime lab had sent us. We met up with the Coroner to get the evidence briefing. The Coroner referred us to the victim's clothing. On the material, the lab had found several traces of rock particles from where the victim landed. Lab also discovered heat mark in the victim's palms which would suggest, that the perpetrator snatched something with extreme force out of the victim's hand causing friction to leave marks. In addition, the lab verified the hair strands found on the body. Lab results showed that the strands belonged to Ms. Peterson. There were strands belonging to a Mr. Honeycomb, and there were also strands belonging to a Mr. Bill Potterson.

The lab also confirmed that when the gun was fired that the shooter wasn't strong enough to hold the gun steady. Due to this, when the bullets left the gun there was a large amount of powder residue that was coated on the ground. Which would mean, that the shooter was not only covered in powder and would have had to wash away the substance, but that there was also a possibility that the shooter's hand could be damaged from the force. This was outstanding evidence! The crime lab hard work could have given us the leads we needed to get this case hot! "Oh, before I forget Doc, I found these pieces of metal out at the crime scene. Also, we found some insurance paperwork. We were hoping you could run some tests on these and get back to us?" Brandon stated. The Coroner agreed to call us when the finding came in.

It was lunch time and I hadn't taken a break yet, so Brandon and I made our way to the lobby to see if there was any food in the vending machines. Inside were a number of sandwiches and some drinks that only contained five percent juice. Well at least I could tell whether it was healthy or not. I was also reminded about Billy statement. The case had gotten so crazy I totally forgot I needed to get his statement before he forgets some of the details. He was a young child and these traumatic events could affect his state of mind. Brandon and I gassed up the squad car and went to pick up Billy, so we could get his account of the crime.

That afternoon, as Brandon and I were approaching the home we pulled up to Billy and the owner of the residence having a shouting match on the lawn, "Whoa! What is going on here?" I directed. Among the "I hate you" and "you're, not my mother" chatter, I was able to pull the owner to the side while Brandon got a hold of Billy crying. "Billy what wrong?" Brandon had asked to try to get the tear to stop flowing. "She scratched me because I didn't want to eat those disgusting peas she cooked," Billy replied. A general response of a rebel who didn't eat peas, but I felt that maybe the whole on the lawn boxing match was a little too much.

Billy had a minor scratch that had a mild amount of blood dripping from them, so we figured we would treat him first. Then we would take him in for a report and we would also treat the owner. We escorted the two to the hospital to be seen. The doctor treated and cleaned Billy's wound, and he was ready to roll. Moments later, the doctor unhinged a chunk of Billy's skin from under the owner's nail.

I could sit here and question why the owner was being so hostile with the little boy, but we didn't have time to dance around. The doctor stated that they would send Billy's DNA up to the lab to ensure that there was no infection and that he should be fine. With a little persuading, I was able to get the owner to calm down and go back to the residence. She assured me that she would be calmer and stubbornly agreed to take haste to the elevator. Back at the office we were finally able to get Billy's report. He could very well be one of the most critical, witnesses in this case. "Hey Captain, we have the young boy here for his statement, and we have more forensic evidence coming from the lab soon" Brandon reported. The Captain looking slightly relieved. We had managed to calm Billy down enough to sit with us after the bribe of a candy bar and something to drink.

"So Billy, I know you are a little upset, but we need your help. Do you think you could tell me what you and your mother were doing before she dropped you off?" I asked this hoping that he would know some information I could use to move forward in this case. "Umm, my mother and I went to the town square. After that, we got some hotdogs and saw Ms. Anderson at the pet shop. Later, my mother took me home and told me to stay there until she got back," Billy said. With Billy finally giving us a statement, it might give us a direct hit on the person Ms. Peterson was going to see. "So Billy, did your mother tell you where she was going when she left back out?" Brandon asked. It was clearly a no by the lowering and rubbing his head. "It ok if you do not know Billy," I replied. He was still unclear about what happened to his mother, but we could tell he was hurt inside from not seeing her for the past couple days.

Brandon and I decided to stop the interview for now and compile the information we did have to see if there were any new clues that could point to the killer. Just as we were preparing to leave the Coroner and the Medical Forensic Division called us to report to the lab. There were able to get the result back. We sat Billy in the lobby to wait on us. The Coroner met us at the stairs and led us down to the lab. As we walked quickly behind her trying to keep up she explained the finding, the Coroner told us that with the help of reconstructive analysis that they were able to reconstruct a digital image of missing pieces to the chipped metal. Apparently, it was a part of a ring? The edges of the metal had traces of gun residue powder on it. This find would strongly support the earlier report about the gun kicking back at the shooter's hand.

This piece of evidence would suggest that the gun kicked back so hard that it chipped away pieces of the shooter's ring. This could also mean that the weapon in question could have scratches from where the ring scuffed against the paint. Even though the location of the murder weapon was still unknown, there was distinct damage done to the frame. Even if the shooter tried to paint over the scratches the difference in paint would still distinguish the gun.

The Coroner continued on to explain the insurance forms found at the home of Ms. Peterson. The forms showed that someone went to a great length to try and change the paper work around. The handwriting was almost a close match to Ms. Peterson, but there were hard differences in many strong letters. Handwriting Analysis Experts viewed the documents and based on the loops of certain letters, and research the lab determined that the writing belonged to a man. The Coroner had given us very strong pieces of evidence. All we had to do was look for a freshly gashed bruise on the suspect hand or a heat burn. This would ensure the capture of the killer. I ran back toward the lobby to check on Billy, and I also needed to brief the Captain.

We escorted Billy back to the car, and as I gripped the steering wheel preparing to leave I thought to myself. "We need to find this Mr. Honeycomb?" I jumped out of the car and ran back up to the office. I quickly asked one of the officers to pull up an address on the man in question. The officer shouted out 1634 Wheel Barrel Road as a possible residence. I quickly raced back to the squad car to take Billy home and made a trip to see this Mr. Honeycomb.

Later that evening, after all the detours were taking care of I found myself parked in front of a white, one story house with pinwheels in the front yard blowing in the wind. This was the place. I was moving so fast I almost forgot Brandon was in the car. "Are you ready," Brandon said. I signal for the move, and we slowly approach the porch. I noticed a television on from the steps. He was in there, and we had a suspect. I rang the doorbell, as my legs tighten up for the unraveling of the suspect. As the door open up and the light from the porch shined bright a woman arose. "Good Evening Ma'am, sorry to bother you this late, but is there a Mr. Honeycomb that reside here?" I asked. She stood there of old age holding a newspaper. As she looked up and her eyes glared open. Her lips began to shift, and she replied.

"Evening Detective, what can I do for you?" Brandon brushing off the delay response asked the lady again, "We need to speak with a Mr. Honeycomb, is he available?" We stood there for a second of silent as we waited for a reply from the lady, was she ok? "Ma'am" I muttered. She began sniffling and with a soft, cracked voice said, "Mr. Honeycomb is my husband, but he has been dead for ten years" My mind rang, and Brandon eyes popped! How could a man's DNA appear on a woman clothing if he had been dead for years? I was at a crossroad, and I didn't know what was going on? We apologized for interrupted her evening, and we proceeded to leave. Driving down what seemed to be a dark, road with no source of light to guide us. We needed assistance from an expert in this matter. Back at the office after the Captain heard the news.

The District Chief had called us to his office. He had gotten the report in on a Mr. Potterson, who was the other suspect in the case. He informed us that Mr. Potterson was a twenty five year old man. There were no criminal record shown, and this guy was a ghost. There were no addresses on file. No phone numbers listed, and even the social security number had been sealed off due to error in the FBI database. There had to be something. The Chief informed us that he would make some calls and try to find out what was the scoop.

We nodded and felt it was time to report in for a snack. I needed something to keep the old body running, because I was feeling the wear and tear. We had been on this case for days now. We had strong evidence, but no linking pieces to a killer. We had names, but some details in reference to the suspects were odd. One was dead, and the other was untraceable. I would not give up though because I owned Billy that. I was going to find out who would hurt such a wonderful woman. With my stomach full of coffee and jelly smeared on my face, I grabbed my briefcase and headed to my desk.

I wanted to review the files, and I needed a quiet place to think. I pulled out the book of notes I had written down and the pictures of evidence the crime lab had provided. So we had a chipped ring. We knew that the killer had gun residue on their hands and possibly their face. We did not have a murder weapon, but we knew it was out there with a very distinct marking on the frame. I also took into account that the killer was a man someone Ms. Peterson knew. And that he was aware of the recent money that she was awarded in life insurance. Plus, there were the burn markings on Ms. Peterson's hand. "Ah" I sighed; we had a lot of work to do. I figure I would go to my car and get my workout clothes. I needed to release some of this mental build up.

I walked down the hall and headed outside to the car to get my short. I had searched my front seat to get change for a drink and noticed rocks on my rugs. "Dang, Brandon dragging rocks in my car; I swept the rocks out, and noticed that some of them were red like the kind found in gardens. Neat rocks, but I need to tell people to clean their shoes before they get in my car.

I put the rocks in my pocket to confront Brandon with later. I was going get payback as I smiled. I started back up the stair heading in the direction of the gym. I noticed a streak of red, lines down the floor. Just then Brandon zoomed pass and I yelled out "You know you are tearing up our delicate floor with these rocks!" as I laughed he looked back saying "This floor is cheap anyway". He was right. This floor was cheap, but it was a good floor. I changed my clothes in the gym and tossed the rocks on my desk. Figure I keep them as a nice, desk design.

After an intense game of basketball, with my team scoring twenty five points to the competition scoring only ten points. Brandon and I went to clean up. We headed back to the office, and we were still waiting for result, a call or someone to come forward. We decided to close up shop. As the day winded down, and we had just finished a quick brief over from the Captain, the State Cemetery called and stated that a grave had been disturbed and that the hands of the deceased were missing?

Upon further details, we learned that the plot belonged to Mr. Honeycomb. The deceased victim that came up in the case we were handling. The state had conducted a service survey that required checking the grounds condition to ensure that the soil was strong, and the plumbing, lawn care and space was being accounted for properly. This information would explain why the hairs were found on the victim's body, but there was no way to tell when the grave had been disturbed. As I heard this horrible news, I thought back to the report that the Coroner had given us.

There were fingerprints on the victim's back? I quickly ran to the Coroner's Office to see if there were prints which I never received. Sure enough the prints on the victim's clothing showed the DNA match Mr. Honeycomb DNA, and there was latex residue smeared on the victim's arms.

This was more detailed information that I did not look over initially, but I knew about the deceased husband, so this information was helpful to a point, but I was still off. The killer must have used the hands to plant another set of prints. I ran to my desk to look back at the notes. There had to be something I did not see. With Mr. Potterson, the unknown suspect still at large, and a number of missing clues I was a little on the edge about this whole ordeal.

As I shuffled through papers Brandon side commented as my eyes zipped page to page, "What are you looking for Mike?" he asked. Clearly I was looking for something, so I nodded and kept to my search. "What up with these weird rocks" Brandon commented as he picked up the rocks in his hand. "Brandon, give me a second," I replied. I could see Brandon staring at the rocks and he was beginning to freak me out! "What is it" I asked, reaching over to grab a rock. "Doesn't this look like blood?" he said. I figure he was dreaming being that these were garden rocks, but I guess I would humor him. I look at the rocks and examine the color closely.

I noticed a strange pattern on the rock that would be probably deemed as coated liquid. I did not see this when I originally grabbed the rocks. It was dark, and I figure it was nothing? "I think you're right Brandon," I replied, but these came out of my car, and I did not know who been in there lately? We ran the rocks to the lab to have them examine. At the same time, the Captain saw us in the hall and asked what was going on due to the speed we were traveling. "We may have found another clue to the case Captain," I said. As we stood there talking with the Captain the red streaks on the floor caught my attention again, and I began to follow the streaks to see exactly where they lead. "Mike, what up," the Captain muttered out. In a dazed, I could hear nothing being said around me.

I followed the streaks up the hall and observed them as they turned passed the water fountain and through a couple of chairs. The trail of streaks led up to the chair that Billy had been sitting in a couple days ago. Could this mean that Billy was there at the scene with the killer and was too scared to tell us? Billy would know who this Mr. Potterson was. I needed to speak with him. I knew Billy might have been scared, and the suspect could have threatened Billy's life, but Billy may have known more details about what happened regarding the murder than we thought. "Captain Waters, we need to go speak with Billy," I shouted.

I couldn't help but think that Billy was being ordered to keep quiet. I knew millions of dollars would push someone to kill and I had seen this to many times not to know. As the Coroner examined the rocks for DNA, Brandon and I took for the residence that Billy was staying. If Billy was in danger, we needed to check on him quick.

It was a little after twelve, and we rushed to the squad car, hoped in and put on the lights (Siren Blaring). Doing about sixty mph through town it took merely moments to arrival at the owner's home. We rushed up to the door and rang the doorbell. "HELLO POLICE, OPEN UP! I shouted. We waited with no response ready to kick down the door. Suddenly we heard a "click" and the door slowly opened. "Yes Detective," the owner answered, shaking as she poked her head around. "Ma'am, I know it's late, but is Billy here," Brandon asked. She nodded, and we entered. Standing there in the front room trembling was Billy.

I could tell he was scared. I had hoped we weren't too late to get answers from Billy. The killer probably already shook the boy's soul right out of his chest. "Billy, we need to talk to you about the night you were dropped off?" I said. He slowly starting to settle down and we all had a seat at the table. "Now Billy, Do you know a Mr. Potterson. We believe he was there when your mother went back out?" Brandon said.

We wanted to find out if this so-called ghost, Mr. Potterson was dating Billy's mother. Billy had replied that he wasn't sure of a Mr. Potterson and that he only knew some of his mother's friends. While sitting there, the Coroner had called. "Excuse me; I need to take this call. Hello Doctor, what did you get for me," I answered praying for good news. The Coroner informed me that the blood found on the rocks was a match for Ms. Peterson's blood. That would mean that Billy wasn't really dropped off, and he was at the scene of the crime when his mother was killed. The killer must have snatched Billy, took him to the house and threaten that if he talked he would be next. He had covered his track well. He also would have been the one that tried to alter the insurance forms.

He was trying to secure a hefty pay off and break town with the money. From what I was gathering this guy was good. No data in the system and no social security number? He might be darn near impossible to find. I was starting to get pissed that this piece of trash was going to outsmart us. I just needed Billy to open up and stop being scared. "Also the hospital called, said that they had some test results back on the owner," she added. I knew she was referring to the "scratch and stiff" outside the owner's home a couple days ago. "Thanks, I will call in a second," I replied. I returned to the table and apologized for my absent.

I checked with Brandon to see if he had any luck getting Billy to tell us anything that could help. He was still tensed and after about thirty minutes of questions, Billy had given us little to go on. All we needed was to find this creep, but it was looking like the killer was going to get away. We still had plenty of time, but we were losing ground. Just then the District Chief emailed me on the National Alert and Police Processing Database. All detectives were required to have this software wired in and downloaded into their phones.

This way, the District Office could reach us if emergencies came about. The email stated that this morning the West National Bank had called to inform Headquarter of a large deposit to Ms. Peterson's account. An amount of one hundred and fifty million dollar scheduled to be deposited in to the bank several weeks from today. How could a dead woman be receiving money deposits? Those accounts were frozen pending further investigation. It seemed that someone had breached access online and hacked the accounts. It had to be the killer making his move on the money! I felt it was time to really sink my teeth in to Billy. Although, he was a young boy he knew the man that his mother was with, and I needed him to crack.

As I was about to dig into Billy my phone began vibrating. I paid it no mind. I wanted this information and I wanted it now. "Billy, you are safe here. No one going to hurt you and we won't allow them to," Brandon told him. Looking as Billy's eyes began watering up.

Maybe we were using the wrong approach, and we needed to ease Billy's mind. Maybe if we distracted him into a different conversation, he might open up. I decided to change the topic and focused on things Billy might have done with him mother. I was sure that fun, past times would calm him down. "So Billy, tell me something you and your mother did when you were younger?" I stated trying to get him to relax.

He followed by telling us about an amazing park they went to a couple years back. And about the food they had eaten on a trip through Paris. As he began to open up I could tell we were breaking ice. Just a few more topics and I would switch to the man in question. Billy wiping his cheeks after several teary eye smiles and colorful, hand gestures later.

I began to see an opening. I had noticed a shiny, spider man ring on Billy's finger. "Hey Billy, that's a cool ring. Did your mother give that to you?" I asked. He nodded, face puffy from tears. "My mother gave it to me for my ninth birthday," he said. After we sat through a moment of dead silence, Brandon had turned and said "It going be okay" Billy finally opened up after I asked about the ring. He began to tell us that the man had seen them walking down the sidewalk. The man called out to his mother, and she had turned around. Billy continued to state that the man and his mother began arguing about some money she owned him.

According to Billy, he used to hear his mother cry about being in debt and that when his father died. She was going to use the life insurance to get them out. Billy also said that the man asked for money and became upset when she refused. He said that the man reached for her, and she tried to run, but he caught her and dragged her across the street. He said that his mother told him to run, but the man pushed his mother down. Shot her twice and chased him through some trees. The man then, forced him to the house and he proceeded to clean his self-up.

The man told him that if he said anything to the police that he would come back and shoot him in the face. He stated that the man forced him to sit on the couch, turned on the television and ran out the back door. "Wow, what a crazy story," I thought. Brandon stood up and patting Billy on the back. "We're proud of you, Billy, you did a great job!" As Brandon and I sat there converting all this into a solid story, and the owner sat there pale as a ghost from the details of these terrible events. I recalled the story in my head. Billy's story supported the details that Mr. Wilson gave us about the figure running off into the shadows.

That must have been when Billy was being chased down by the suspect. I could see most of the details of the crime fitting. Now Brandon and I had to find the suspect. As we headed to the door I slowly turned and ask Billy one last question. "Do you know where the man is now?" I said. He looked up at me and said he wasn't sure, but he said he remembered his mother saying something about going to the mountains.

We had plenty of evidence, and we were going to catch this guy. I leaned over to Billy and thanked him for being so strong and helping us. "Hey Sport! You might want to take care of that amazing spider man ring, it starting to chipped," I said to Billy. Brandon looking back at us "Yea, you wouldn't what to mess that up, it was a gift from your mom," he added. As we took our leave, I told the owner to have a great night, and thanked her for allowing us into her home as we headed to the car. I glanced at my phone and noticed that I had a missed call from the hospital, but it was pretty late and I wasn't sure if I wanted to bother them.

Brandon and I sat in the car sharing each other thoughts on the crazy way all this went down and recalled the details that local shared. We reviewed the story that Billy told us. We had an eye witness and several side witnesses. The case was strong, and we were going to crack this open. That sick pervert just attacked her and then harassed a child. It made my blood boil. The team called us in to give us the data on the bank's transactions. It was so late, we decided to just crash in the car.

Bright and early the next morning before the birds started chirping. Brandon went in to the office while I grabbed us something to eat. A couple of biscuits ought to do the trick. I needed to compare my notes with the previous ones in my books. As I enter the building, a strange feeling came over me. How did this man get into town and no one saw him? No ID check at the bridge, Nothing! I was blown away and yet in still I was determine to catch him as if I knew exactly where he was.

I was starting to think that our suspect was somebody that already lived in town, but I had never heard of a Bill Potterson before? If the suspect had left town we would have surveillance footage of it. I met Brandon up stairs, and we sat down at our desks to begin our compare and data entry.

As we reviewed the stories I begun to see details in certain reports that didn't add up and where was my murder weapon? We now knew that Mr. Potterson had to be our suspect. But how did he escape without being seen?

The plot of this case got thicker and thicker. "Mike, the District Chief wants to see you," Brandon muttered from around the corner. I jumped up and proceeded to the Chief's Office. I wondered what he could need this early.

There I stood in the Chief's doorway waiting for him to speak. "Good Morning Chief, you needed to see me," as I signaled the Chief of my present. His waved me to come in and have a seat. He hung up the phone and told me that he wanted a report on where we stood in the case? If there was any new evidence and if we had obtain any leads to the whereabouts of the suspect? I informed him of what we did have and that we were preparing a Tactic and Defense Team to send up to the mountains. He was impressed but not completely satisfied. We needed a criminal behind bars to pay for the crimes that he committed. As I headed back to my office to meet up with Brandon, I realized I never called the hospital back. I decided now was a better time than any. I wasn't swapped with piles of paperwork.

(Ring Ring) "Good Morning Water Bridge Hospital, this is Susie, how can I help you," a lady so sweetly answered the phone. "Yes, this is Detective Mike Hallman from the Downtown Police Headquarter Office, and I received a message from the lab yesterday?" She paused to do what I assumed was check out the call logs. She replied with a yes, and then transferred me to the lab's main phone line. I was greeted by what sounded like a sweet, petite, young lady. She informed me that the doctor had received the test result back, and the lab showed no infection.

It also showed that the DNA found under the owner's nails belonged to a Mr. Potterson! . . . . I WAS SHOCKED OUT OF MY PANTS! The DNA found under the owner's nails was the skin of Billy Peterson. How in the world could the DNA be a match to Mr. Potterson? I asked how accurate the test was.

The young lady replied that the test was ninety nine percent accurate. I didn't want to alarm any one, so I called Brandon and informed the Chief of the hospital DNA results. Maybe there was a mix up with the blood tubes. They did get shipped across the water to a lab for processing. I told Brandon to meet me at the corner of Orchard and Baker Street. This had to be a mistake, but I felt that I should check out all the possibility and view the report details that the Coroner had provided for us. I had a black light in the trunk of my squad car and other crime scene equipment. I figure I would bring it in to see if the reports were right about the crime scene.

If Billy was the real suspect in this murder his hand would be damaged, and he would be covered with residue from the murder weapon. We drove to the home and exited the vehicle. The owner was standing in the door. "Hello there Detectives how are you," she said waving from the porch. As we walked up I glanced over to see Billy in the window with his face pressed up against the glass.

He gave us a look of death. Like fear staring at you. I looked back toward the owner and informed her that we needed to speak with Billy. He was now gone from the window. Brandon and I made entry into the home and called out to Billy. There was no response and even though he was a boy, we had to remain guarded. We made our way through the hall to the back room to find Billy sitting at the coffee table "Hello Billy, we need to talk to you again," Brandon called out to him as we inch toward the chairs. Billy snatched his head up and replied "Why?" Sitting down I pulled out my books and the crime kit I retrieve from the car. There was no damage to his hand that I could see. "Billy, we need to talk about your story," Brandon said, started up the conversation with Billy. I began to open up the case. "Billy, remember when you told us that the man dragged your mother? Well, we checked that out, and your mother was never dragged," Brandon stated as I pushed my chair back.

We knew that it wasn't true because there were never any drag marks reported. I observed Billy's ring again and noticed the chipped pieces. The same chipped pieces that I noticed before. "Billy, can you tell us what happened to your ring and how it got chipped," I asked. He stated that he dropped it in the street a long time ago. Brandon indicated that the story he told us wasn't true and that we believe he damaged the ring a different way. Billy started to shake saying that we were liars and to go away. I rose up over Billy and pulled out my black light. "Billy, this is a black light, and it's going show us if there is any dust on you?" I said to him. I turned it on and swept the light across Billy's hands and chest . . . . There was powder! I couldn't believe it.

I jumped back to reach for my weapon as Brandon rose to his feet. The owner gasped, and Billy looked up at me. "So Detectives, I guess I'm going to jail" It was Billy, he was the killer? The suspect earlier revealed by DNA as Bill Potterson. He tricked everyone into believing he was a little boy, but how was the question I wondered? We called in the Defense and Tactic unit and had Billy escorted down to the station for interrogation. We reported to the Chief's Office to brief the squad on the situation. We had found our killer, but what happened? I needed to get the truth from the perpetrator. It was early the next morning and we headed back to the precinct. Brandon and I entered the room. "Bill, that your name correct, says here you're twenty five years old?" Brandon began to say as we sat down. "Why'd you do it?" I said. Like we didn't already know exactly why this piece of gunk did what he did. After several hours in the interrogation room, Mr. Bill Potterson confessed to the murder of Ms Ruby Peterson.

According to the reports written by Detective Brandon and I, the alleged suspect preyed on Ms. Peterson and pretended to be her son, when discovering that she had married a rich oil vice president. The suspect had an aging disease that allowed him to pose as her son using medicines and other methods to fit the son description.

The suspect had tried to alter the insurance will and living will to transfer all fund into a fake account under the victim's name. A total of four hundred and forty two million in estate funds, and three hundred and fifty millions in life insurance money was pending approval. Once Ms. Peterson was out of the picture all the funds would be passed down to her son, Billy. The suspect had inside help from a source at the FBI, and a Bank Teller at West National. The two alleged suspects are under Federal investigation. The suspect gave detectives false information to throw them off the case, but thanks to great police work the killer was brought to justice. After further investigation, over the course of the next week, the Search and Rescue Team discovered the remains of the real Billy Peterson buried on the outskirt of the city's wood lines. The suspect was charged with two counts of murder and was facing life in prison.

We still didn't know where the murder weapon was, so we decided to go to the neighbor's home to look in the one place that we never checked. Billy's bags were sitting there in the house and with not even an ounce of suspicion. I then rally the troops I could and headed to the house. On site at the home, detectives and police task force scouted the area. In Billy's bag crime specialist found a black, nine millimeter handgun and several bullet casing. There was a vapor conceal rub that covered marks and cuts on the skin, which would explain why I didn't see any damage to the suspect hand. There was also a large, cold, foil wrapped object stuffed in the corner of the bag. Upon opening the wrap police found an ice case with the missing remains from Mr. Honeycomb's grave. The latex gloves that were used, a pack of syringes and a peel mask applicator were also found in the back of the bag. With the murder weapon located we had all the evidence needed to lock this creep up.

We notify the Captain of our finding and finished searching the premises. As the day passed and the crime team began wrapping up, the Chief called to let us know that the suspect was in holding and was ready for transport. He needed to be process and took to booking, so I jumped in the car and took to the station before the others headed out. There were still vague details on the money transfers. I checked in with Captain Waters and the District Chief, finalized my report for the in-processing

Office and then headed to holding to secure the suspect. I wanted to find out where the money was and get whatever documents he had stashed away. There was no pay off for this jail bait.

As I walked up to the holding block, I signaled the guard to unlock the holding cell and unlatched the gate. As the door opened and the light from the hall lit up the room, my stomach was bottomless to what I had observed. The suspect, Mr. Bill Potterson, was gone as if he had just walked through the walls. "Where'd he go," I yelled at the top of lungs. "Sound the alarm," I kept yelling as I ran down the hall and around chairs. The suspect had escape, and I could not figure out how? There were steel doors, sensor panels, strong hold gates, and a decent upgraded building with an ample amount of cameras. How would he have gotten out the cell let alone made it out the building? (Siren Whaling) We had dispatched several units and a SWAT unit to search for the suspect before he got too far. After weeks of flipping over every rock known to man, it would seem that the suspect, Bill. Potterson was gone.

The case was put in a pending status as the search for our suspected killer continued. A few weeks later, we were able to locate family of Ms. Peterson to inform them of the tragic events. A few days later, the families arrived in town to attend the funeral. As ushers brought out the casket and set up for the ceremony. Many of the family members wanted to see the victim to show their respects. We advised the ushers to do showings under strict supervision so that everything remained calm and peaceful. The usher opened the casket, and to their utter shock there was no corpse inside! "Ah!" people began shouting while several fell to their knees. 'What going on?" I screamed running to the front to view the commotion. I was shocked. I called the Coroner's Office immediately and alerted her of the missing corpse. There was no explanation.

She was dead to my understanding and here before my eyes laid an empty casket. This case was strange even for a crazy person to grasp. I radio Brandon in order to shed some light on my thinking. Maybe I was drowning in cases and wasn't focused. I was done in by the weight of this case, and the suspect had eluded me? We ensure the families that we would uncover this bizarre situation. Upon a detailed search, the missing body was found and after further review into the DNA back at the lab, we had discovered that the body wasn't real and was constructed with special chemicals, fake organs and materials in order for it to seem real. Also, when we checked with the owner of the funeral home, he reported that none of his guys were on shift at the delivery time of the body.

And we later found out that the suspect had set up a deal to have a master key passed off to him inside the jail. Police later found, there was an inmate's cell with the window bars gone, that he apparently escaped through.

I headed back to the office to meet with the District Chief, and the Commission Board of Police Safety was also present. We had been played, and the Board went on to address the level of urgent work that needed to be done. There was untraceable money, a missing victim and a suspect that was possibly more ingenious than any we had encounter. This roller coaster had to be dealt with as soon as humanly possible. We put our full effort and best people on the case and left it in the hands of God. After the board meeting, the bank had called the Captain to inform him of a wire transfer hold and reroute of funds. The bank had received an image and print out from a partnering bank in the island four thousand miles north of our current position. The West National Bank had put Ms. Peterson's funds on high movement alert after the recent events.

It seemed the partnering bank out in the island had a man and woman enter the bank earlier that day and withdrew a large amount of funds. The bank's figures also showed several million dollars transferred to different account under the name Billy Peterson. The bank had sent the image to the printer. We waited for the finished image to come through and there walking hand in hand, in the bank smiling together as if to say "got you suckers" was Ms. Peterson and the alleged suspect and killer Mr. Bill Potterson. It was a scam!? It appeared that it was a setup and, she did it to get the money. She ran off with the suspect to live the movie star life. Detective Brandon and I went to the home of what use to be the

27

Peterson's residence to search for any clues to nail these monsters. "Check her Voicemails!" I yelled out to Brandon. Maybe there was something explaining the crime.

There had to be some self-destructing evidence on these tapes. We pulled all the tapes and after fourteen hours of recordings. We stumbled onto a message of Ms. Peterson and the suspect conversing about the events of the crime and how they planned to killed Billy in order to trigger the life insurance claim.

She would then have him assume the identity of Billy and fake her death in order to have her life insurance money paid out. The policy that covered Billy which he would have received on his eighteenth birthday, and the policy covering her to provide Billy support in the event of her death. These policies along with her late husband's company insurance would put her in an early retirement. It continued on about how she was sick of taking care of Billy, because he was spoil rotten and she wanted her life back. The tape revealed details of her affair with the suspect and how they planned everything.

The tapes even revealed that the death of Ms. Peterson's late husband was a part of the plan. It was a shame. The reckless idea of people's will to kill for a simple piece of paper. Just for a breath of fresh air or a break? Instead of enjoying a walk in the park to ease the nerves, she brutally had her son and husband killed in cold blood. What a lady, but I would never put anything passed a corrupt mind. You never know what goes on in the mind of a killer. They were ghosts. But I had a job to do, and I was going to catch the criminals who spilled Blood on Orchard Street.

PART 2

THE MAN IN THE BLINDS

Detective Mike . . . . Detective Mike . . . . DETECTIVE MIKE! "Huh?" I said snapping out of a trance. "You have a phone call Mike," said Brandon. I nodded and notice the transfer icon on the phone lighting up. At this point, it had been a year after the investigation and by this time I was finally taking a break from the case. Some friends and I had planned a spa, resort getaway. I couldn't wait to dive in the shimmering, clear ocean water. It was at a great time too being that Brandon was transferring out of state for a police training course. He was going to be gone for a couple weeks, and I didn't know what I would do without my partner in crime. Ironically enough I smiled. The District Chief had been transferred to a different department, and the Captain had taken medical leave. The office was quiet, and the cases didn't come in as heavy. I had taken that from all the moving trucks passing by the building that there were several new neighbors.

The police force usually welcomed all the newcomers into town just to show some warm hearted love. Maybe we would do something for them once everyone returned. With how slow the office was running now would be a great time to get a little air. I headed to the park, wind blowing across several small, puddles of water and blades of grass. It was peaceful and just what I needed to clear my mind. The events from the case were still bothering me, and I wanted to solve this crime. I wouldn't let this case get under my skin. As I walked through the park pulling on loose, tree branches that were hanging out, I noticed a couple sitting on the bench. "Hello guys, how are you doing," I called out. They greeted me, and I walked over to introduce myself.

They smiled and told me about their journey to our little town. The couple was from the north and had two kids. "Nice to see some people smiling," I commented. Just as the conversation started getting interesting I got a page from the office. (Radio Sounds) Unit car four, three, three, three, we got a disturbance call coming from Baker Street. Please be advised caller location, address one forty two, four people in the home, condition non—hostile. (Radio Sounds End) As I reached for my radio to reply to the call, the couple stated that they just moved in over that way. "I will check to make sure everything ok folks. You guys enjoy this weather," I said heading to the car. I put on my sirens (Siren Blaring) and took for Baker Street. As I pulled up to the reported caller's location I noticed a moving truck unloading across the street. "That must have been where the couple was staying," I thought to myself. I hoped out of my vehicle and made my way to the porch.

I swiftly knock on the door "Police," I stated. The door quickly swung open and a lady anxiously started talking about some blinds and a man in the window. Needless to say, I was a little lost, but I was willing to try and decode. "Ma'am, calm down and slowly tell me what's going on," I said. She began to state that there was a figure in the window across the street. She said that she was on the porch, and someone had cracked open a piece of the blinds. All she could see was a finger and an eye staring at her. Feeling uncomfortable she observed the peeping eye hoping that her looking back would scare the person to close the blinds. She went on to say that the person continued to stare at her and moments later blood starting running down the window. I was a little shocked. Her story was quite the spill. I looked across the street, and of course I didn't see anything off, and I didn't want to just run over and start pointing fingers of blood leaking windows and strange peeping eyes!

They were new to the town and the last thing I wanted to do was scare them off within the first few hours. I told the lady I would check into it and to call me if anything strange happened. She quickly nodded and I stepped off the porch looking back and forth. My eyes wandering and thinking "Could this be a joke?" I had never heard anything like this and to be honest it was a bit of bologna. I didn't want to accuse the lady of being a crazed, lying nut job, but this kind of call needed more proof. I walked to my car shaking my head. I took a long deep breath and gave a sigh of anything but relief.

To my surprise the Captain had called and gave me the following day off. He thought that I needed a break, and I hadn't really had a moment home to relax. This was true and I gladly took the chance at getting some downtime. Maybe I could see when this whole amazing trip was. I could see it now, on the beach drinking cranberry swirls, tequila and lime, tall bottle of rock house beers and chasing girly up the strip. "The perfect detective's vacation, secretly that is," I laughed. I knew that I needed to lock up the office, so I swung by the building, grabbed a couple of useful tools, some paperwork to review while I was relaxing and locked up. "I might need to add some colors to this place," I thought. Sure would feel a whole lot better in here if I had some life. It was so dull and bland.

After loading up the car I smashed the pedal for home. As I drove passed the park I couldn't help but notice the couple still sitting at the park. "Wow, they must really like the outside," I thought. As I drove pass I tried to focus on the road, but I couldn't help feel like someone was looking at me. I turned back toward the park with a speedy eye as not to crash and noticed the couple staring at me. It was creepy.

They stared and stared. Even after I looked they continue to stare. It was a weird moment. I felt as if they were disgusted with this look of a hateful neighbor. I didn't pay it much mind though seeing as they were new here. Maybe they were the kind of people that just like to stare. When I arrived home, I kicked off my shoes, heated up the oven and turned on the newly, purchased sixty inch television. I imagined this would be the place where all the magic would happen if I was social with any of the ladies. I worked so much I didn't even remember women existed until a commercial came on showing a woman on the beach. Oh, how I would love to be the man holding up her bra straps," I thought as a clever grin slowly made its way from one ear to the other. I figured I would shower and take a quick nap.

Several hours passed, and I awoke sprawled out on the couch and food still in the oven. "Dang, dark outside, must have been sleepy then I thought," as I rose from the couch and stretched out the kinks. I didn't even eat after that shower. That cold water felt like clouds of soft, hand stitched pillows lifting me to a sweet slumber. I headed to the kitchen to eat what was possibly left of the burned pasta I heated up. I usually kept the oven on low for safe heating. Just on the offset chance I fell asleep. It wouldn't be the first time I done it. Luckily for me the food was still edible, and I was starving. We made a great team and I planned on sending this food straight to the cleaner.

I sat down on the couch and searched through the channels to find a good show, when I saw in the mirror what appeared to be a shadow in my back window. I turned faster than a cheetah without breaking my neck. "Hey, who's there?" I screamed. The shadow began to move away from the window. I didn't know who it was, but I was convicted it was a prowler, and I was ready to protect my home. I grabbed my handgun and made for the front door. I barreled my way out the door and headed to the backyard. As I continue to yell out trying to brush out the prowler, I ran to the sideway. There was no one around my house, but I wasn't crazy. Just then I turned to the end of the street and saw a figure standing there under the streetlight. "Hey Police! Who's goes there," I shouted. I started down the sideway picking up speed as I got closer and closer. Still a couple houses away, the strange figure started to come into focus.

Suddenly, the figure sped off around the corner. "HEY!" I Shouted as I began to run faster and reached the end of the block. I looked around, and the strange figure had vanished. I was running off of adrenaline, and I couldn't bring my heart to a calm pace. I was pretty shocked by the situation. I had never had a problem with prowlers in the neighborhood before.

I radio the station to send out a unit. I ran inside to grab my keys and headed to my car. I shot around the corner and alerted the precinct to inform dispatch of a possible prowler. That I was going to patrol the area. After an extensive search through a number of streets, all I was able to find was a crazed cat, a bunch of late night drinkers and a broken lamp in the middle of an alley.

The other patrol cars reported a domestic scene, a loose dog and a bunch of kids in the street playing with water hoses. There was no prowler, and I feared I was too late. He had gotten away. I doubled backed around the corner and as I passed Baker Street I had noticed that the new neighbors were still very actively unloading. "Wow, they must have had a lot of stuff?" I thought to myself. I started to slow down curious about the statement the woman gave me earlier across the street. I knew it was totally weird, but I couldn't help but wonder if there was something there.

I pulled off to the side of the road. I waited for a second to observe the home and everything seemed normal. There were lights on and people unloading. I couldn't find anything strange about that, and I usually could tell weird from just mistaken vision.

I started to inch forward as I prepared to pull off when I noticed the blinds cracked open. Glaring back to see who was there it seem to be a small finger poking out. I stopped and rolled down the window a bit to get a better view. Just then a face appeared in the blind. I couldn't see perfectly from that distance, but I have a well enough view to notice something strange.

There was an odd, shaped shadow behind the face and just as I contemplated getting out of the car. The face was ripped from the window. "What the hell," I thought, as I swung the vehicle around. I jumped out as I put on my lights (Siren Blaring). I radio in to dispatch. "Dispatch two—two—one. I have a possible domestic scene, standing by for back up confirmation" I waiting for them to response before I approach the house. (Radio Sounds) "Go for Dispatch two-two-one, possible domestic in progress, we have multiple units on standby (Radio Sounds End) I walked up to the house as the occupants stepped out onto the porch.

The couple began to address me. "Hello Detective, is there something wrong?" I stood there for a second to listen for noises and adjusted my belt to stall time. "Sorry to bother seeing as how you guys are still unpacking, but there a prowler loose and I wanted to make sure everything was okay".

They stated that they were fine and were almost finished unpacking. "Ok then, be careful out here," I said as I walked back to the car. I radio in a disregard to the call and decided that if something was going on it was minor. Maybe it was one of the kids in the window, and somebody pulled them off? Although that wasn't the best thing to do it's not a crime to get upset at kids for messing up good blinds. I headed back to my house and decided to quit before I drove myself insane. I was going to call it a night.

The next day as I made my way to the office two squad cars were called out to a robbery in progress. We had dispatch tracking the progress of the call, when all of a sudden one of the officers radio in (Over the Radio) SHOTS FIRED, SHOTS FIRED! Officer down, Officer down suspect is armed and extremely dangerous (Radio Ends). I was quickly alerted to the incident in progress and several units, Tactic and Defense Unit and I were dispatched to the scene for back up. On arrival at the location in question units set up and the Defense unit got into position. The suspect was standing in the middle of the street dripping blood with what appeared to be chrome colored firearm. There were shell casings everywhere, and people were hidden behind any object they could find to avoid the wave of bullets.

The Defense Team began setting up blockage on every surrounding street as a patrol units brought out the loud speaker. "Drop your weapon and get on your knee!" the officer called out. The suspect standing there said nothing. Was he thinking about if he wanted to continue the killing? We couldn't take any chances and allow more people to get hurt. The suspect had shot one of our own and we couldn't let this go on any longer. The officer repeating to the suspect to dropped the weapon. Still refusing he raised his hand and wiped the blood from his face.

It was the husband of the couple I met at the park. I was stunned to see him standing there! He had seemed fine the other day, and here he was with a gun. I grabbed the loud speaker and advised the man to drop the weapon. There was nothing, he was cold and non-responsive. We knew we had to get the gun away from the suspect but how to move about without causing any turmoil. Just then the man raised the gun to his chin and fired . . . .

The crowd has fallen weak to the images just witnessed. He had killed an officer, and upon further view in the bank there was a teller who was shot. The senseless killing that I had witnessed was beginning to become a trend and I was sick of it. The Coroner and Medical Forensic Team had been called to secure the crime scene and retrieve evidence. The Coroner collected all the materials needed to conduct the investigation. The medical report showed that the suspect was Jonathan Potterson, the brother of Bill Potterson, who was a contracted hit man for a top secret federal underground sector. The evidence also showed that the bank teller that was killed was the teller that was under investigation in the previous case involving Bill Potterson.

We had been working on trying to get all the information we could and possibly cut the suspects involved a deal for the whereabouts of Bill Potterson. He was untraceable and now we suspected he was sending his brother to kill off loose ends that would possibly trace back to him? He was beating us to the resolution in this case, and I had to stop him before we had a cold case. The only remaining suspect and person involved in this case was the source at the FBI. If we were right, he was coming after the last person that was a potential threat to finding him. I had to inform the District Chief and the Captain immediately! After the streets were cleared up I reported the details to the Police Commission Office and Border Patrol.

A global search warrant was sent out for the arrest or details on Bill Potterson. It was apparent that we had to locate the two suspects as large. Dispatch sent units to the home to bring in the wife and kids. Units were to search the home for evidence and bring them in for questioning, but as police units approached Baker Street from a distance they could see smoke and flames.

The house was on fire and crumbling to the ground. We notify Fire and Paramedic Teams as precaution stated to have medical assistance on site. After drowning the fire out the Search and Rescue Team bowled through the initial level of rumble looking for bodies of surviving victims, but there was only wood and debris. They were not there. But upon a deeper search into the rumble, the bodies of the two children were found. One of the child's throats was sliced. That would explain the blood covered window the lady reported and the other child had burned to death in the fire. A Radio dispatch unit came over the intercom informing all units of a possible threat to the FBI building. There was an unknown vehicle outside in the parking lot. Detectives and local units in the area zoomed over as reports of the West wing lot being the intended location came over the radios.

Police were on site and closing in on the suspicion vehicle. Units moved in from each angle on the target. Detectives in the office had learned that the agent in question worked out of that office and may be a target. Federal agent assisted in the breached of the vehicle only to notice in the reflection of some water underneath the vehicle, a red light blinking, and numbers flashing across the ground. BOMB!!!!!! Get back someone yelled out as a flock of agents took off for cover. Meanwhile, back at dispatch there were calls coming in about a woman on the fifteenth floor with an assault rifle.

The bomb was a diversion. Agents headed for the elevator to secure the remaining floors, but it was jammed. As dispatch stayed on the phone trying to keep agents and police units on the ground up to date on the pending situation, sounds of gunfire static hit the phone lines. There was a cut out, and the calls were lost . . . .

(Rumbling Noise) The bomb had gone off and the parking lot along with a huge hole of damage to the first floor had been done. The remaining suspects in the Bill Potterson's case had been killed. The woman was still on the floor as far as we knew, and agents had tried to access the elevator. There was still no luck, and she could possibly kill more innocent bystanders?

The chances of getting to her were slim as ground units tried to figure out some kind of strong attempt. As police converse in the street fifteen stories above them glass began to fall, and a body fell out of the window. Not a second later, the pavement was covered in blood, and police identified the body as the wife of Jonathan Potterson. A young woman named Mrs. Patty Potterson, a young tropical florist. Strange that a florist would kill herself just to get to and kill some random agent? Unless they knew each other and there was something I wasn't putting together? Was there a connection to any of this? Officers and the Police Headquarter held a ceremony for the loss of a fellow comrade.

The next day after the ceremony, the District Chief had returned to the station and was furious about the news. The bloodshed was enough to make even the strongest stomach shake. We had no idea what we were going to do to stop this mad man? We had to formulate a plan to get this guy. The arrest warrant didn't turn up anything and people were too afraid to call if they did know something. He was a menace. A cold blooded killer and was capable of anything.

Finally after all the searches, defense teams and countless hours gathering evidence the Border Patrol with the help of State Troopers, caught up with Bill Potterson. According to the report sent to our office, Potterson accompanied by Ms. Peterson were spotted by a local bar tender who fished in his spared time. He just so happen to spot the couple a few miles off the shore of a beach. He then called the Crime Hotline and had given law enforcement detailed descriptions of the two suspects. He stated that he noticed something about the couple that stood out like he had seen them before. A closer look revealed that it was the woman police were looking for. The strong makeup that the suspect wore was a dead on detail in the recorded call which was able to lead detective to an arrest. The suspects were flown back to the Police Headquarter across the water.

I was called from the plane and informed of the suspect's arrival. I verified the time and went to handle a long list of damaged property and inventory of weapons. A few hours later, I was instructed to report to the airport and transport the two criminals into custody. Shortly arriving ten minutes before the expected landing time, I smacked open a magazine and sat patiently. I couldn't wait to see these low lives, bottom of the barrel, cold blooded pieces of dirt. I wanted to laugh in their faces. They thought they had outsmarted us and had gotten away with murder, but we were going to find them no matter how long it took.

As the plane docked and lowered the ramp, I looked us to see Ms. Peterson when she exited the plane. I couldn't believe that I had known this woman so long and she was a pie baking, murdering monster. I had begun to walk in the direction of the suspects when; Suddenly, Ms. Peterson reached for the gun in the guard belt's holster. Everything and everyone around me had slowed down. She began to slowly lift the gun and pointed it toward me and several officers. I could hear the famous lines being yelled as guns began to be drawn.

"Put down the weapon now!" a guard shouted. I moved up toward the suspect and shook my firearm. "Please put down the weapon. You don't want do this," I said trying to reason with her. She began to tremble uncontrollably, and the weapon began to make a clicking noise as her finger hit the trigger well. "I'm not going to jail!" she screamed. I hated to rain on her untrained idea that this was going to end like some of the movies did where the perpetrator got away, but it wasn't. She was going and she knew it. "I'm sorry Ma'am, but you can just kill people and get away with it," I stated. She aimed the gun at me, and I fired . . . .

The second suspect then reached for the gun, and a second shot was fired. They were down, and it was all over. I was speechless. A once potentially cold case had turned around, and the killers were caught and brought to justice. I was relieved but empty inside. That was it; all of it.

Homeland Security and Department of Transportation had escorted all personnel and pending passengers of any scheduled flights out of the building. All flights were temporarily suspended. I walked out to the front of the building to find Brandon, the Captain and the District Chief along with other members of the police force were all standing there waiting for me. "Are you ok?" Brandon said. I was happy to see him. He didn't know the half of what had been going on since he'd been gone. Everybody greeted me and headed inside to handle business on clean up, witness statements, weapon inventory, collect prints and get the Coroner's Office ready for pick up.

Weeks later as thing started to calm down from one of the most disturbing cases in the history of our archives. I couldn't help but wonder what happened to the money, and why did these individuals go through so much only to end up with nothing in the end. I wanted to know more about this woman and the history behind her? Maybe that would tell me something?

The following day I decided to go to the library and look up on a well-known site that displayed people family history and birth places. I typed in Ms. Peterson name and up popped pages of family trees, history, relatives names listed by marriage, blood and all the children in their blood lines. Even Brandon's name had showed up on the page! Of course, you couldn't access these files without clearance to personal data and paying a fee deemed by the provider of the website. So with my curiosity I paid the required fee to view the files. The site requested the user to enter in credit card information and the pop up prompt allowed you to view your account to verified funds available. My account had indicated a pending balance deposit of over five hundred million dollars! "Whoa!" Racking my brain it seemed the money had being sent to my account? "What was going on? I pressed ok to clear payment, and the page came up of all the children. Although some files were restricted, it stated that Ms. Peterson had birthed two sons.

Billy Peterson was the younger of the two boys. The page continued on to state that Ms. Peterson was married many years ago to a level—two computer technician. I had heard about level-two classified project. She had birthed her oldest son at a local hospital that was burnt down many years ago. I remembered that hospital because I had investigated the burning of that place. They lost everything. As I ran down the page, I began to see more names. It showed the name of Ms Peterson first husband, a Mr. John Hallman! The couples had a son named Mike Hallman . . . . !!!??

My arm had gotten weak, and I was unable to scroll the mouse . . . I soon found that all the names in the archives were those of all the people that were involved or murdered in the case of Bill Potterson. There were all relatives of mine. I had killed my own mother . . . . and Bill was my stepfather. I was always told I was an orphan. I was sick. I ran out of the library and hoped in my car. I drove like a maniac to Orchard Street. I stop, exited the car and stood in the place where it all had started.

I was confused but cover with guilt. My phone rang. I looked at the screen dripping tears of pain onto the lining of the phone. It was Brandon. I picked up crying "Hello," I answered. 'Hey Mike, is everything ok. I haven't heard from you in a while?" he said. I told him no and that I was a murderer. It was time for me to go and that I had solved enough murders. That I felt it was time for me to cause one. As I said goodbye I could hear Brandon yelling wait from the phone, I threw the phone to the ground and smashed it until there was only a reflection showing of me on the screen. I pulled out my gun and placed it to my face. As tears slid down the barrel I wondered what it would have been like to have known her, but it was too late. I pulled the trigger. That was it. All of it

Now I had spilled blood on Orchard Street.

PART 3

MEMORIES OF A DYING LOVE

". . . . Mike . . . . I miss you" . . . . Mike was gone. I didn't know how to handle it. I didn't even know what made him do it. He was my partner for years and now I was sitting at his funeral. The Coroner's report stated that Mike's body was recovered on Orchard Street. A single bullet was found lodged in his skull. He had bled to death. Doctors said if he would have made it to the hospital; there was still a chance he could have lived. "Brandon, are you ok?" I heard the Captain ask as he walked up from behind. I was barely hanging on, and there were so many thoughts in my mind. I guess I had to live a new life. With a new mind and a truly dim view on what sanity translated to.

The next day, the Police Headquarter held a memorial for one of the most extremely well rounded detectives to grace the force. I decided that I could not stay on the force anymore. I needed to get out of this town and take some time to deal with everything that had happened. I met with the District Chief to discuss my options of leaving, but he would not let me quit the force. He instead felt that I could take as much time as I needed, but I was still a part of the team and that he would not lose two of his best detectives. I gracefully agreed and after a week of out processing and paper work transfers. I packed up my bags and took off.

Thousands of miles away in an old, red cabin located outside of a wooded area, I drunk myself into a coma of liquor that had burned the inside of my heart and spread like a fire in a pool of gasoline. I would never be ok, but I would try my hardest to wake up the next morning without tears falling from my face.

It had felt like weeks, and the next day as my eyes opened, and I kicked the covers off my waist. I received what was probably the most bizarre phone call ever. (Ring Ring) "Hello Detective Brandon," I answered. "Hello Detective Brandon, this is Bell, Bell Hallman. I was told to contact you in case of an emergency" I jumped up, voice box apparently missing, because I tried to speak and nothing would come out. "A . . . A . . . . , Are you Mike's sister," I muttered. She said yes, and I rose to my feet.

How did she get this number? How did she know me? I was quite taking back at the moment that I couldn't even think. She told me that her and Mike had found each other a few years back and had told her to call me in the event of his death. He had put a lot of men in prison, and he felt that his sister wasn't safe so he never mention her to anyone. With the birth of her beautiful newborn a few years back, she felt the danger of her life had slowly risen. I could understand the need for hiding. From time to time criminals had outside sources to do their dirty work.

I didn't know what to say. I felt a little dry. I had a piece of Mike back, but under all the wrong circumstances, but if I was needed I was not turning my back on her. "So what can I do for you Ma'am," I replied. She began to grow soft in her voice and informed me that two days ago a man followed her into a store. She was concern that their lives were in peril. She had managed to lose the man in a crowd just a few blocks from the store. I had agreed to help and fly out to her home. I couldn't let anything happen to her. I owned Mike that, he was like my brother.

The following day instead of the well planned out vacation. I had hoped the fastest flight several hours back to a remote city north of my home town. When I arrived I met up with Bell in the airport's food section. I could distinguish her from all the other women around. She had the glow of a soft, beautiful angel. Her lips were plush, pink, and her hair was a long, wavy brown. She was amazing, but I needed to stay focus on the intent of my visit. I was there to protect a young woman and her baby. "Hello there Miss Bell," I nodded greeting her with a kiss on the hand. A smile arose, and I was introduced to small, wrapped toddler.

I was uneasy to such a warm welcome in a public place, especially to a woman who was a possible target. Something wasn't right, and I felt open. Without making a scene, I quickly viewed my perimeter of the people around me. As my eyes turned passed a small table, I noticed a light shimmering off a man's leg underneath a newspaper. It was a gun, and that was Bell's stalker.

The hit was in effect as I stood there making small talk with the possibility of being shot in the face at a moment notice. There would be no warnings and no way to avoid the hit. I slowly pulled her close and whispered in her ear as not to alarm the man of our escape plan. As she began to shake slowly, I could feel her heart beat start to speed up. "Don't worry; we will be fine," I said. With people all around me, there was a need for a subtle run, but it was a perfect move. I quickly glanced over to the man's table to see him peeking over the paper, and I grabbed Bell's hand. The chase had started, and it was a life or death outcome.

The toddler dragging from her hips as we ran through the food court and pushed the gears of my feet to over drive. I wondered about stopping to think, but there was no time for brain work. The man had barreled from the chair as the newspaper flew over the—caution wet floor-sign and a chrome, long nose silencer rose from his side. I had to make decisions in a time frame that I wasn't sure the brain could operate.

I looked back to see if a hand and kid was still attached to my body. I could feel the soft grip of a hand, so I was sure she was still there. I couldn't let the rush confuse me. As I glanced back to pin point where the unknown man was I had a vast lead on him, and we were looking good, just then Bell began to give way and her soft hand was beginning to slip. I couldn't let her go. "Hold on Bell, I shouted pulling her to a nearby cart. I pulled my firearm, flipped open my phone and loaded my clip in to the well. I instructed Bell to dial nine-one-one! As I looked over the edge of the cart I could see the man was standing a few hundred feet away, thankfully at this point people were running and screaming.

They would keep us hidden long enough to make it out of here. As Bell relayed details to dispatch I swung out from behind the cart and fired one shot at the man's chest. "Ugh," I heard from around the cart. I had hit the suspect, and a few moment later local police had arrival at the gate. Secured the area and took what was hanging on of the suspect's life to the hospital.

After treatment was provided to the suspect's wound, and he was stable, a local officer and I enter the room. "So who are you?" The officer asked. I stood there itching to get my claws into this guy. I wanted answers! He was an apparent hit man hired by someone to take out Bell, but she had been in hiding for years. Who could have known she was here? I left the officer to his work and headed for Bell.

There was something that I needed to ask and that could be the possible eye opener to this whole crazy chase. "Bell, I got to ask you a question?" fixing my jacket. She turned to me in a panic and grabbed my hand in relief. "Yes, what is it?" she replied. "Have you met anyone or made any friends since you been here?" Leaning over as I caught my breath. She paused and thought hard. A few second later she recalled a woman at a hair parlor. "What was her name?" I asked.

As she began to calm down a little more, she stated that the woman last name was Peterson! I knew something was wrong, but why would a Peterson be after Bell? I needed to call back home and touch base with the Chief. Maybe he would know something that could explain the reason why? I got Bell and her little one to a safe location so I could call.

"Police Headquarter, District Chief speaking," the Chief answered. I informed the Chief that it was me, and I needed to find out if there were any details in Mike's crime scene report. If there had been any weird information that had anything to do with the name Peterson. Being that the Chief was the only one allowed to certain files.

He told me that based on the site's information Mike viewed, the victim, Ms. Peterson was Mike's biological mother and that Mike had a sister named Bell, and also a sister named Molly Hallman. Upon Mike's death, Bell would receive all of Mike's inheritance. If the recipient was not able to claim the estate then the next of kin in line would claim the estate. That being Molly, but no one had even seen let alone heard of Molly? Bell was shocked. "Molly! I have another sister?" She yelled out. I was confused though. Why would people be coming after Bell for?

The Chief continue on to state that before Mike's death the file he had accessed on the site required personal information. Bank transactions showed that Mike had a balance of over five hundred million dollar deposited into his account.

With the help of a computer team, they were able to trace the source of where the funds came from? The point of origin showed the transfer came out of the island where Bill Potterson was located. That was all the information the Chief had at the moment and was trying to get more. After listening to the Chief, it was obvious that someone was trying to take out Bell to get to the money. I didn't know who though. I needed to find out what was going on. If they were sending hit men after Bell stopping more of them from coming wasn't going to solve this problem. We decided to relocate and move somewhere a little less in the open. We were sitting targets.

We sat down and put our heads together to figure out what was the motive behind all this running. Just at that moment Bell's phone began ringing. She couldn't recall ever seeing the number before. Alert to the situation a little more, I told her to pick up and put it on speaker. "Hello? Who is this?" she began speaking softly, anxiously numb to the strange caller. (Deep voice on the phone)" . . . . You have something I want Bell . . . . your mother failed to get me what I wanted. "What do I have, and who are you?" Bell asked. (Voice continue) . . . . you have my money . . . . I am the devil, and I am going to kill you and everything you love". The phone clicked, and the call ended. Her heart sank, and several tears began to roll down her face. She was scared out of her mind. Who was this creep? We had to figure this out. Her child had grown hungry, and we had to eat. Just as the waitress approached the table a loud noise had breeze shut my ear, and a bullet had blown it way through Bell's child head. "No!" She cried out falling to the ground.

I dived over to shield her, and we slid under a bigger table that blocked the direction where the shot had come from. "It's a sniper, stay down!" I directed. I was blindsided, and I didn't even notice anything out of the ordinary. Her child was dead, and I had failed her. I was supposed to protect her. But I didn't protect the baby. The only thing she still had left, and it was gone. I couldn't even process the pain she was feeling, but I did know that we had to move from the spot we were in or the next bullets were ours.

. . . . As people scattered I leaned over to scout a way through the tables. I looked up to see if I could get a visual of the shooter. Luckily for me the sun was bright enough that it shined a light from the shooter's tip. A glare gave me an open shot that I refuse to miss. I tried to calm Bell down enough to explain the plan for a distraction. It was a dangerous move. I didn't want her to get hurt, but I needed something. "Bell, give me your purse!" I quickly muttered. Maybe she had an item in her purse that I could use. If I could throw the shooter's attention out of focus for just for a split second, I had a possible shot? I looked inside her purse and found several small items including a small can of hair spray, a pack of matches and a roll of papers.

I instructed Bell to wrap the bulk of papers around the can, tuck her strap inside and light the cloth material on the inside of her purse on fire. On the count of three, she was to throw the bag to the next table as fast as she possibly could. Bell tossed the purse crying as she could see the body of her child lying across the ground. Police were in the general area, but weren't able to move in without locating the position of the sniper.

As the bag began to melt I could see the paper, wrapped can start changing colors. It was about to blow, and my chance of taking a shot was closing in. I told Bell to put her head down and looked away. The pressure from the heat exploded the can and adjusted the shooter's eye. I quickly swung my gun and one eye out just enough to catch the glare. I took a deep breath and pulled the trigger all in a swift motion and roll back under the table. I waited for a sign of some sort or something to confirm my shot, but we had to move. I grabbed Bell's hand and bolted for the car. I figure that from the lack of bullets zipping across my face I had landed my shot. In a panic and dripping sweat we quickly jumped in the car. Bell fell ill from the lack of weight on her waist. There was nothing holding her down. No hand gripping hers.

Police had secured the area several minutes later after getting the clear on the shooter. The run was breaking me down. I was trying to be strong for Bell, but I couldn't hold up much longer. I needed a break, rest and a reason to keep pushing forward. "Are you ok Bell?" staring at her as she sat there shaking? "You did a great job Bell, thank you for your help," as I tried to comfort her. She nodded as a thank you and we drove off. There was a beach house that the police department used for witness relocation. I figure we could head there to duck out of the gunfire. It would take some time to get there, so we needed to pack and get anything we felt was important. I looked forward to the long drive. It may have been just what the doctor ordered.

. . . . On the road . . . . , the ride had calm me enough to think. It was late and I didn't know what was running through Bell's head as she put all the alarming information she was just informed of into a thought. She was quiet. Losing a child, learning that she had a long lost sister and that there were people after her for millions of dollars that she didn't even know about? It was a load to take in. I waited for her to speak. I figured she would need a moment to collect herself. Hours later we pulled into a wide driveway with a two story beach home.

Maybe I would get half of that vacation after all. Bell took toward the bathroom to clean up while I checked outside for any strange or unsafe surrounding. Suddenly, I heard a loud noise coming from inside the house. I ran up to the door and heard Bell screaming. "Get off Me!" she was shouting at the top of her lungs. There was someone here. I leaped up the stairs and ran to the door of the bedroom with my gun drawn. I sneak a peek in, and there was a man standing over Bell with a gun pointed at her face. I stepped into the room; "Hey, let her go!" I yelled as I observed the suspect's clothing. I could tell he was one of the hired help. There was no way to get away from these guys. Everywhere we went they beat us to the punch but how?

There had to be a tracking device or something that was attached to Bell. "Ah, come in detective, I have been waiting for you," the man said. I told him to let her go, or the result would not end well. "Oh, detective I can't do that, you see Bell here in the sole recipient of my money. I have Molly hostage with all her information and banking data and upon Bell's death all the money will be transfer to Molly's account which in turn, will be sent to me! The money that her mother owned me!! I was putting the pieces of why these people were after her together, but I was unfamiliar to any of the other details. "I'm sorry, but I can't let you leave here alive," I said. He stated that was not my decision, and he was leaving. Clicking the hammer back with the intent to kill I knew I couldn't let this happen. I shouted out "FREEZE!!!!" distracting the man and starting shooting every bullet I possibly had in my gun clip. As he fell riddled with bullets, oddly enough he was able to pop off two shot into Bell's leg.

After the suspect was down I ran over to Bell shivering on the bed and losing blood at a fast rate. Grabbing her and rushing downstairs to the car, I applied a thick cloth to her leg and called nine-one-one and informed the hospital I needed a police room setup for a gunshot victim. I just prayed that they would be able to save her. Being chased by professional hit men had distance my mind and I had never got back to the Chief. I called to inform the Chief of what had happened on my end, and that I was at the hospital waiting as the doctors worked on her. I told him that I would be probably coming back early. It was too much going on, and I couldn't function anymore. Everywhere I went there was a murder.

I hung up with the Chief and went in to check on Bell's condition. She was in a critical state, and the doctor's report stated that she was hit in a main artery. She was going to die. I was able to see her at this point, but the time was short. I held her hand for all of five minute. I told Bell that I was sorry and that I had failed her and I had also failed Mike. I told her that I was going to find Molly. Her last breath that was taken ended with a stream of words that I didn't expect. "Tell him I knew and that I'm sorry I didn't tell him. Tell him I love and miss him and tell him that you're ok," she said "That I'm okay," I wonder? Her eyes rolled back, and she gripped my hand tighter. "I love you brother" There was silence. As I unwrapped my hand there was a balled up piece of paper. It was my birth certificate. It showed that my mother was Ms. Peterson, the victim that turned out to also be Mike's mother.

. . . . She was my sister! I cried as I held a broken heart in my hands. I had died. There on the bed laid two battered and destroy lives. Bell's life and mine . . . .

This meant that Mike was my real brother. I couldn't feel my leg, and I had gone blind. I sat there dying inside wondering what I had left. I had to locate Molly. She was my little sister, and I had to find her. I didn't know if she was in danger, but I needed to find some sort of clues. I figure that the dead man's body back at the beach house would hold something since he had her held somewhere. I headed back anxiously with a thousand different ideas surfing through my mind. I could barely keep the wheels on the road. This whole time Mike had been my brother. What else didn't I know? It took a while, but I finally arrived at the house. I ran up stair to the body lying on the floor and began looking for a phone, a note or some kind of evidence that would tell me where Molly was. I was pacing while my body stood still. I checked his pockets, shoes and all. I had found the phone, a wallet and a picture.

The picture I had found was of a woman and two small children. It must have been his family. The wallet had an ID and cards everywhere. The man's name was Walter M. Small. The man I was told was my father! The picture that he had in his wallet was one of his wife and my other siblings. I was disgusted. My dad was the one who had shot and killed my sister. I couldn't let this twisted and crazy train continue. I had to stop this madness. I headed for the car and pulled out my computer. I ran the number that was last called through a reverse look-up and found that the call came from a toy factory out in the country. I knew that's where Molly would be! I was going in this alone, but I was nervous. I had no idea what would be there and if Molly was even still alive.

Several hours later I pulled up to the building. This was the place. I was certain of it, but how did I get in without being caught. Just then I heard people talking. I noticed an open vent that was big enough to fit through. I quickly dove in and close the vent behind me. I crawled to the end of the pipe which had put me over where Molly would have been. I looked down the vent opening and saw her standing there. I had to help. I took a second look around as I slid the vent cover over and poke my head out. When the coast was clear, I jumped down onto a high stack of steel cases. I slid out to a pole that lead to the ground and roll over behind Molly. There were plenty of cases by the pole, so I had a good place to hide. "Molly," I whispered.

The woman's head snapped back toward me. She looked confused and scared. "Are you Molly?" I asked. She had shook her head yes, and I began to inch forward. As I grabbed the tape, I told her that I was her brother and that I was going to get her out of there.

I tried ripping the tape around her hands but couldn't. I knew that if I tried to pull the tape from her mouth it would hurt, so I grabbed my gun. I cocked it back a few times empty, slowly enough so that it wasn't loud, but enough to heat up the tip. I then told her to be very still, and I burned a hole in the middle of the tape. "What is going on here?" I asked. She told me that a man named Walter Small kidnapped her saying something about his money.

That he would hold her until her mother paid him and that she better come up with the money soon, or he was going to kill her. I needed to get her loose. I looked for a nearby item that I could use to cut the tape. I spotted a small piece of glass on the floor. I picked it up and sliced Molly free. "Well. Walter dead and he killed your sister, Bell. I said moving toward the wall. "Come on, we need to get out of here"

"No, Brandon I am not going anywhere, I'm sorry," she said. I stopped and turned toward Molly. I was confused. What was going on with her? I told her that she was in shock and that we had to leave. She looked at me and pulled out a black remote. She pressed a red button on the remote and a machine had grabbed me by my arms and legs. "I'm sorry, Brandon, but I'm not leaving because I have everything I want and there is no one to stop me! Do you know what it likes to have nothing! To grow up and have nobody around to care about you! To be abandon by the woman that is supposedly your mother. I was going to get what was owned to me. That freaking punk, Walter tried to push in on my business, but you took care of that for me.

He was so stupid. All I had to do was find a way to trick him into thinking Bell was in the way, and he was getting stiffed. I didn't want to get my hands dirty. You see, mother and Bill owned Walter money from a business transaction they made with my product. But they messed up and failed to get the money.

This in turn, would have cost me a loss that I couldn't afford. So mother married some rich man to scam out of the money they owned Walter, and we formulated this brilliant plan to get everything they possibly could. They even killed Billy for his insurance policy. Eventually, they had got greedy from the potential profit and decided to snake Walter out of his money and keep it for their selves. Little did they know that Walter had people everywhere and had found out their plan? So they tried to cut their losses, transfer the money to Mike's account and dip off the radar for a while, but thanks to living in a small city you can't keep that kind of stuff a secret.

Your police department and Mike took care of them as well. I needed people to die for the cause, and that was easy since little Jonathan would do anything for his little cousin. I even got his wife involved. Dying was a part of the risk they took.

I was there at Jonathan's house while they were unloading. I had to make sure everything went accorded to plan, but I just couldn't trust the children. Darn shame about his little ones though, but they were going to open their big mouths and ruined all the work I had done. So I had to get rid of them. Everybody else just kind of fell in to place and I made sure that I kept Mike on his toes.

And poor little Bell, the only little heifer standing in my way of getting all of the inheritance.

So of course I had Walter fooled to take care of her and with him and her out of the picture. I would be the only living relative to claim the funds. It was pretty easy! And as far as all the money goes I was the one who hacked the accounts at the bank. I needed to wait for the right time and transfer the entire amount to a secure stock.

If any money hit any account that belonged to a family member the funds would be rerouted, and all the money would be deposited to me. The money would never be traceable again and it would disappear off the grid. See the reality of this is that everyone was working for me. They might not have known it, but I just manipulated what I saw fit, to ensure that, in the end, I was the only one still alive. I would make everything looked like a series of crazy murders or suicides. So now, all that left is you!" As my legs begun to go numb I couldn't believe that my own little sister set up to scam, and kill our whole family for some inheritance. "How much Molly, how much was it worth!" I screamed, coughing from the lack of blood flowing through my body. "Oh Brandon, it was only a mere eight hundred million or more, but the best part about all this is there more.

I'm sure you are wondering what these tanks have inside them. Well, this is a highly toxic nitrogen acid. It will burn the skin off of a human body in ten second. Very dangerous and highly expensive! The market is booming for this stuff. My yearly profit from this alone is at 7.5 billion dollars. Well, I'm sure by now your body has stop pumping as much blood. I am sorry about this, Brandon, but I can't have any loose end". I struggled hoping for a miracle, but it was over. I was going to die.

This case had taken a mind blowing turn, and I was the next victim. It was a good run, but it was time to turn in my badge. I laid my head down. "I hope you can't feel anything because this is going to be painful. Goodbye Brandon" She pressed a green button on the remote and acid had begun pouring over my body.

The acid had burned through my hand, and I screamed as my body began to feel like fire was punching my organs out. Molly walked away laughing as I fell to the floor. The machine's chains had melted, and I was dying at a rapid pace, but before I died I would avenge my family. My body let me do the impossible and I had one shot left to shoot. "Hey Molly, hope you can't feel anything," screaming in horrible pain I squeezed the trigger. She fell to the floor gasping for air. I would die knowing that she was going to die to.

. . . . Now I could sleep and dream of my brother . . . .

About the Author

Charles Morst
A Crime Novel Writer

Charles Morst was born in Hampton, VA 1988 The young author is a residence of South Carolina This book is the author's first crime book in the Fierce 8 collection entitled *"Blood on Orchard Street"* *2013*

Made in the USA
San Bernardino, CA
13 November 2013